W9-CKI-606

Volleyball

• An Introduction to Being a Good Sport •

by Aaron Derr

illustrations by Scott Angle

RED CHAIR PRESS

Start Smart books are published by Red Chair Press

Red Chair Press LLC   PO Box 333   South Egremont, MA 01258-0333
www.redchairpress.com

Publisher's Cataloging-In-Publication Data

Names: Derr, Aaron. | Angle, Scott, illustrator.

Title: Volleyball : an introduction to being a good sport / by Aaron Derr ; illustrations by Scott Angle.

Description: South Egremont, MA : Red Chair Press, [2017] | Start smart: sports | Interest age level: 005-009. | Includes Fast Fact sidebars, a glossary and references for additional reading. | Includes bibliographical references and index. | Summary: "Playing a sport is good exercise and fun, but being part of a team is more fun for everyone when you know the rules of the game and how to be a good sport. Volleyball is one of the most popular sports around the world for both boys and girls. In this book, readers learn the role of various positions and how to set up the court."-- Provided by publisher.

Identifiers: LCCN 2016934119 | ISBN 978-1-63440-134-0 (library hardcover) | ISBN 978-1-63440-140-1 (paperback) | ISBN 978-1-63440-146-3 (ebook)

Subjects: LCSH: Volleyball--Juvenile literature. | Sportsmanship--Juvenile literature. CYAC: Volleyball. | Sportsmanship.

Classification: LCC GV1015.34 .D47 2017 (print) | LCC GV1015.34 (ebook) | DDC 796.325--dc23

Illustration credits: Scott Angle; technical charts by Joe LeMonnier

Photo credits: Cover p. 5, 7, 8, 13, 14, 20, 21, 22, 27, 28, 29, 31, 32: Dreamstime; p. 32: Courtesy of the author, Aaron Derr

This series first published by:
Red Chair Press LLC   PO Box 333   South Egremont, MA 01258-0333

Printed in the United States of America

Distributed in the U.S. by Lerner Publisher Services. www.lernerbooks.com

1116 1P CGBS17

Table of Contents

Words in **bold type** are defined in the glossary.

CHAPTER 1

Something New

Trisha and Sabah are best friends. They hang out together. They do their homework together. They walk to school together. They do almost everything together, except for one thing. Trisha is on the volleyball team, and Sabah doesn't know *anything* about volleyball.

Sometimes, Trisha invites Sabah to come to volleyball practice. Trisha is good friends with the other members of her team. But Sabah always says no.

Sometimes, Sabah is afraid to try things she has never tried before. What if she messes up in front of Trisha's friends? What if she makes a mistake because she doesn't know the rules?

"It's no big deal," Trisha says one day. "When I first started playing, I made lots of mistakes. But now I love it!"

Sabah thinks about it one more time. "OK, fine," Sabah says. "I'll try it. But just this once." "Yes!" says Trisha. "This is going to be great!"

FUN FACT

Volleyball was invented by a man named William G. Morgan way back in 1895!

It was originally called Mintonette.

CHAPTER 2

The First Practice

"OK guys," says Trisha's volleyball coach. "We have a special guest today. Her name is Sabah, and hopefully she'll have so much fun practicing with us that she'll want to join our team."

"Yeah, Sabah!" all the members of the team say at once.

Sabah just smiles.

DID YOU KNOW?

After the ball is served, each team can touch it three times before hitting it back over the net. But be careful! The same player cannot touch the ball twice in a row. If a player doesn't hit the ball over the net, she at least tries to hit it just right so a teammate can hit it over the net. If the ball touches the ground on your side of the court, the other team gets a point. If you hit the ball **out of bounds**, the other team gets a point. If your team hits the ball four times in a row, the other team gets a point!

The first thing the players work on is serving. Their coach explains that the goal of the **serve** is to hit the ball over the net. It's tricky because if you don't hit the ball hard enough, it might hit the net. But if you hit it too hard, it might land outside of the **boundary**.

Both of those things are bad for your team. Expert volleyball players usually try **overhand** serves. They toss the ball high in the air with one hand, then jump up and slam them ball over the net with the other hand.

But this takes a lot of practice. For now, the players on Trisha's team are working on **underhand** serves. They hold the ball in one hand, then they turn their hand so the ball starts to roll off.

But before the ball actually leaves their hand, they swing their other arm up and smack the ball over the net.

FUN FACT

Volleyball games start when one player serves the ball by hitting it over the net with a hand or arm. Then the other team tries to hit the ball back without letting it touch the ground.

"OK Sabah," the coach says. "Now it's your turn." Sabah is nervous.

She holds the ball in her left hand, then she turns her hand to the side and lets the ball roll off. Then she swings her right hand up … and hits the ball right at the coach!

Sabah is embarrassed.

"That's OK, Sabah," says Billy, one of the other players on the team. "You'll get it. Just keep practicing."

Sabah keeps working, over and over, until finally she hits one over the net!

"Great job," says Allison. "That was a great serve!" Sabah just smiles.

JUST JOKING!

Q: What can you serve, but never eat?

A: A volleyball !

Each volleyball team uses six players at a time. Players line up in two rows of 3 players. The server stands facing the net in the back-right corner of the court. If her team wins the point, she gets to serve again. When the team that isn't serving scores a point, the players on that team rotate so someone else gets to serve.

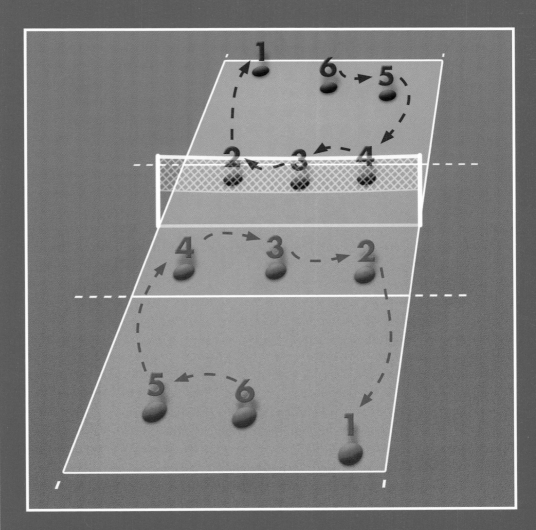

CHAPTER 3

Learning the Skills

Next, the players work on **passing**.

When the other team hits the ball over the net, it's a good idea to try to pass it softly to a teammate. This gives your team the chance to get in position so they can really hit one hard back to the other team.

It's good to hit the ball hard over the net, but the pass to your teammate needs to be nice and easy.

Trisha's coach shows the players how to hold their hands together and straighten their arms so it looks like the letter "V." Then they work on letting the ball bounce off the bottom part of their arms so it goes softly up in the air.

When it gets to be Sabah's turn, the ball bounces off her hands and hits her right in the face!

FUN FACT

In volleyball, you can't catch the ball. Instead, you have to strike it so it bounces off of your hand or arm. If you catch it and throw it, the other team gets a point!

Indoor volleyball became an official Olympic sport at the 1964 Summer Olympics in Tokyo, Japan. The Soviet Union has won the most indoor volleyball gold medals in Olympic history. Beach volleyball, which is played outdoors in the sand, became an Olympic sport at the 1996 Olympics in the United States. The United States has won the most beach volleyball gold medals.

"That's OK," says Amad. "The same thing happened to me when I first tried. Keep practicing and you'll get better."

On the second try, the ball bounces off Sabah's hands and drops straight to the ground. On the third try, the ball sails way back over her head and out of bounds.

But on the fourth try … Sabah gets it! The ball bounces off her arms and flies softly through the air.

A perfect pass!

Next, the team works on **setting**.

After a player makes a good pass, the next player to touch the ball usually tries to set it up for one last hit. But the plan only works if the players use good teamwork.

The setter usually tries to hit the ball with both hands above her head. The coach tells the players to push the ball up in the air without catching it.

The first time Sabah tries, she accidentally hits the ball out of bounds.

"Good try, Sabah," Trisha says. "Keep practicing."

Sabah just smiles and gets back to work.

JUST JOKING!

Q: What's a volleyball player's favorite city?

A: Volleywood!

VOLLEYWOOD

CHAPTER 4

Working as a Team

Next, the team works on one of the most exciting plays in volleyball: the **attack**. Some people call this the "**spike**" because you really get to spike the ball hard over the net. If the other team can't hit it back, it's called a **kill**.

A good attack is only possible after a good pass and a good set. It takes perfect timing and lots of practice.

The players work on their attacks by jumping in the air and swinging one arm up at the ball. They try to hit the ball with their hand hard enough that the other team can't hit it back.

Sabah is so excited that she hits the ball too hard and it goes way out of bounds!

JUST JOKING!

Q: Why is volleyball so dangerous?

A: Because there are so many spikes!

A **fault** is when a team or player goes against the rules and the other team gets a point, like if a player catches the ball or hits it two times in a row. If a server crosses over the boundary line when serving, that's a fault. If a player touches the net during a game, that's a fault, too!

"That happens all the time," the coach says. "It's OK to hit the ball hard, but you have to stay in control, too."

Sabah tries again, and this time her attack is perfect!

"Great job!" her teammates say.

When you're trying an attack, it's a good idea to aim for an area where the other team doesn't have any players.

Sometimes, attackers will even try to trick the other team by hitting it super soft over the net. They usually aren't expecting that!

FUN FACT

Volleyball games include sets and matches. In most leagues, the first team to score 25 points wins the set. But the game isn't over yet! Depending on your league, you usually have to win two or three sets to win the match.

The last skill the team works on is blocking and digging.

A **block** is when a player jumps up and blocks the other team's attack. A **dig** is when a player has to lean over real low to hit the ball. It's kind of like you're "digging" the ball out of the ground.

Trisha's team spends the final part of practice working on blocking and digging.

DID YOU KNOW?

An "ace" is when a player makes a super serve and the ball hits the ground on the other side of the net before being touched by an opposing player. Some servers are so good, they can make the ball curve as it flies through the air!

Sabah realizes that volleyball is pretty simple once you learn the rules. First, you serve. Then the other team passes, sets and attacks.

Then the other team blocks or digs, and sets and attacks. This is called a rally.

And it keeps going until the ball hits the ground, goes out of bounds or hits the net!

You have to have good teamwork, and you have to get plenty of practice so everybody knows their job.

"I think I'm starting to get the hang of this," Sabah says.

JUST JOKING!

Q: Why is the dog so good at volleyball?

A: He's a good digger!

CHAPTER 5

The Big Game

"**W**ell Sabah, we have a game this weekend," the coach says when practice is over. "Would you like to join our team?"

All of the players look at Sabah. But she's not embarrassed. She's ready to play.

"I'll be there," she says.

"Yes!" Trisha cheers. "This is going to be great!"

At the game, Sabah and Trisha realize that the other team is pretty good. It looks like they've been practicing hard, too.

"OK team," Sabah's coach says. "Just remember to try your best."

When it gets to be Sabah's turn to serve, she accidentally hits the ball right in the net. When the other team tries to spike the ball, Sabah misses the block. And when Sabah tries to make a pass to her teammate, the ball goes out of bounds.

But she isn't about to give up. "You can do it, Sabah!" her teammates say.

The next time it's Sabah's turn to serve, she smacks it right over the net! And when the other team hits the ball back, Sabah makes a perfect pass to one of her teammates.

At the end of the game, Sabah's team needs just one more point to win the match. The other team serves the ball, and one of Sabah's teammates makes a great pass to Trisha.

Trisha then sets the ball up for Sabah, and Sabah jumps up and spikes it over the net.

The ball hits the ground! Their team has won the game!

"Good job, Sabah!" her teammates say.

"I knew you'd like volleyball," Trisha says.

And Sabah just smiles.

If you want to become a good volleyball player, you need to work on serving, passing, setting, attacking, blocking and digging. But you don't have to do it with a real net in a real gym. Just grab a friend or trusted adult and take a ball into any grassy field. Have your friend throw the ball at you in different spots and at different speeds. Practice hitting the ball back without catching it. Work on aiming the ball so you know where it's going to go. Work on tapping the ball high in the air so you'll be able to set up a teammate in a real game. And, finally, work on serving the ball at different speeds and heights.

Glossary

attack: a hit that should send the ball over the net onto the other team's court; also called a spike

block: jumping up in front of the net with your arms in the air, trying to block the other team's attack

boundary: the outside edge of the volleyball court; a ball that lands outside the boundary is out of bounds, giving the other team a point

dig: when a player must lean over or even dive low to stop the ball from hitting the ground

fault: when a team is unable to hit the ball back over the net under the rules of the game

kill: an attack or spike that hits the ground and is not returned by the other team

overhand: hitting the ball with your arm raised above your head

out of bounds: when the ball lands outside the boundary

pass: when a player hits the ball into the air so a teammate can set it

rally: the part of a volleyball game that starts with a serve and ends with a fault

serve: the first hit of a rally, when a player stands near the back of the court and attempts to hit the ball over the net

set: a play that sets up a teammate for an attack

side-out: when the receiving team gets the ball to serve whether earning a point or not

spike: a hit that should send the ball over the net onto the other team's court; also called an attack

underhand: hitting the ball by swinging your arm up from below your waist

What Did You Learn?

See how much you learned about volleyball. Answer *true* or *false* for each statement below. Write your answers on a separate piece of paper.

1 On the third hit by the same team, the ball must go over the net.
True or false?

2 The same player can hit the ball only twice before someone else must touch it.
True or false?

3 Every rally starts with a serve.
True or false?

4 A team gets a point when it commits a fault.
True or false?

5 Beach volleyball was invented long before indoor volleyball.
True or false?

Answers: 1. True, 2. False. (The same player can hit the ball only once without a teammate touching it.), 3. True, 4. False. (The other team gets a point on a fault), 5. False. (Indoor volleyball came first.)

29

For More Information

Books

Giddens, Sandra. *Volleyball: Rules, Tips, Strategy, and Safety.* Rosen Publishing, 2005.

Suen, Anastasia. *A Girl's Guide to Volleyball.* Capstone Press, 2012.

Places

International Volleyball Hall of Fame, Holyoke, Massachusetts. International, college, and Olympic exhibits in the city where the game was invented.

Web Sites

Kidzworld: Playing Volleyball- rules and history
http://www.kidzworld.com/article/4963-playing-volleyball

Volleyball Advisors rules and strategy
http://www.volleyballadvisors.com/how-to-play-volleyball.html

Note to educators and parents: Our editors have carefully reviewed these web sites to ensure they are suitable for children. Web sites change frequently, however, and we cannot guarantee that a site's future contents will continue to meet our high standards of quality and educational value. You may wish to preview these sites and closely supervise children whenever they access the Internet.

RULES OF THE GAME
FOR YOUNGER PLAYERS

1. Most school-age teams have 8 players (not 6).

2. The height of the net is usually set at 6 feet 6 inches for younger players (about 7 feet 4 inches for older players).

3. Servers may stand up to 10 to 15 feet inside the baseline (*older players stand behind the baseline*).

4. The youngest players may toss the ball over the net to serve (*versus using an underhand serve recommended for most younger players*).

5. If a server has 3 successful serves in a row, the ball goes to the other side to serve; no point is awarded for this **side-out**. It's just fair play to switch sides.

6. If the serve hits the net and goes over the net, but is not put into action by the other side. The serving team gets a point.

    If the ball hits the net but does not go over, the result is a side-out and the other team is awarded a point.

7. The first team to score 21 points, while being ahead by a minimum of 2 points, wins the game or set. A team must win by two points or reach the maximum of 25 points to win.

Index

About the Author

Aaron Derr Aaron Derr is a writer based just outside of Dallas, Texas. He has more than 15 years of experience writing and editing magazines and books for kids of all ages. When he's not reading or writing, Aaron enjoys watching and playing sports, and being a good sport with his wife and two kids.